Weekly Reader Children's Book Club presents

Maude and Claude Go Abroad

By Susan Meddaugh

Houghton Mifflin Company · Boston

This book is a presentation of Weekly Reader Books.
Weekly Reader Books offers book clubs for children
from preschool through high school. For further
information write to: **Weekly Reader Books,**
4343 Equity Drive, Columbus, Ohio 43228.

Published by arrangement with Houghton Mifflin Company.

Library of Congress Cataloging in Publication Data

Meddaugh, Susan.
　Maude and Claude go abroad.

　SUMMARY: While cruising to France, a sister
and brother go overboard and encounter a whale
who is being pursued by harpooners.
　[1. Brothers and sisters – Fiction.　2. Whales –
Fiction.　3. Stories in rhyme]　I. Title.
PZ8.3.M55115Mau　　[E]　　79-26460
ISBN 0-395-29162-3

For John and Debi

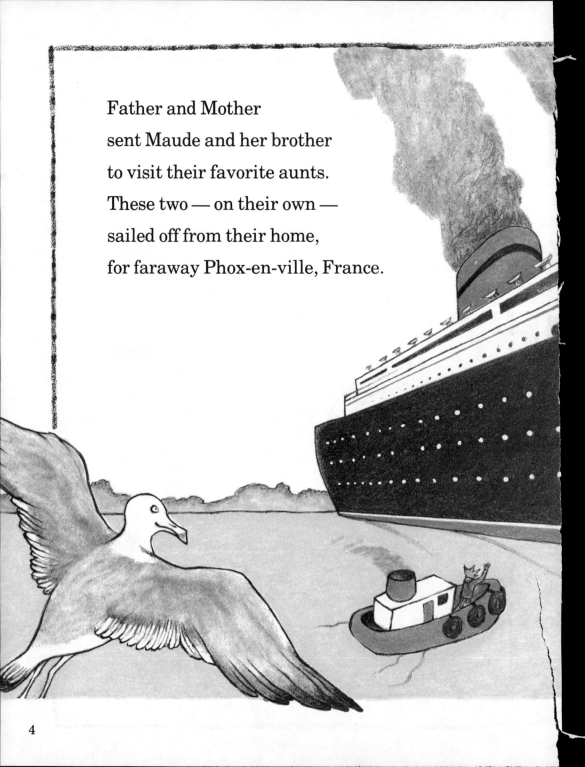

Father and Mother
sent Maude and her brother
to visit their favorite aunts.
These two — on their own —
sailed off from their home,
for faraway Phox-en-ville, France.

"Take care of your brother.
You haven't another,"
said Mother to Maude who was older.
"Please keep him in sight
all day and all night."
"I promise I will," Maudie told her.

The porter took Maude
and her brother Claude
to a room that was theirs for the trip.
"This stateroom's a great room,"
said Claude. "I can't wait
to explore every floor of this ship."

Claude had to inspect

every spot on the deck.

No nautical nook was neglected.

Sighed Maude, "This is hard.

The S.S. *Reynard*

is far bigger than I expected."

Unfortunately,

on the third day at sea,

Claude ran off alone to the stern.

And as they were sailing,

he climbed up the railing

and balanced there feeding a tern.

Maude knew in a flash,

when she heard a big splash,

that her brother had gone in the water.

What else could she do

but jump over too?

For Maude was a dutiful daughter.

13

Claude giggled, "What fun."

But Maude was undone.

She looked up and said with dismay,

"I'm glad you can float,

because there goes the boat."

And they watched as it sailed far away.

Then up from the deep

rose a mountain so steep,

a creature of towering size.

He looked out of breath

and half scared to death.

"A whale!" Maudie said with surprise.

She cried, "We are saved!"

She shouted and waved.

The whale only gasped as he passed her:

"I'd stop if I could,

but I can't, for it would

surely lead to an awful disaster."

17

"A ship under sail

is hot on my trail.

The crew on this ship has one notion.

They don't think of me

as king of the sea

but as valuable blubber in motion.

"I'm beat and I'm busted.

My insides are rusted.

I'm tired and I've had a spoutful!"

"We'll help you to hide,

if you'll give us a ride,"

Maudie cried to the whale, who looked doubtful.

"We'll sit on your spout

so no water comes out.

We'll look like we're sitting on dry land.

Submerging your tail,

you won't look like a whale.

You'll really look more like an island."

The big fellow gazed

out over the waves.

His spout spurted short nervous squirts.

Then he said, "I'm willing."

And Claude said, "How thrilling!"

And Maude said, "I do hope this works."

Maude heard the whale gulp
as the whale ship sailed up.
She felt a small tremble run through him.
A cruel-looking creature
with menacing features
leaned over the side and said to them:

"Avast there, landlubbers!
We're fast after blubber.
Have you seen a gray whale today?
We were right behind him,
but now we can't find him."
And Maude said, "He went thataway!"

24

Then Maude heard him hiss,
"What island is this?
I do not recall it at all.

I'll look it up later
for we cannot wait or
our profits will be much too small.

"So, full speed ahead!"
the mean captain said
to his scurvy old crew on the schooner.
The whale with delight
watched the ship sail from sight,
and with it each nasty harpooner.

"How can I repay you?"
he asked. "Did you say you
were rideless?" And Maudie replied,
"We're due at our aunts'
in Phox-en-ville, France,
and we certainly could use a ride."

They sailed to the east

on their stately old beast,

sunny days, starry nights in slow motion.

And as they were cruising

the whale told amusing

and colorful tales of the ocean.

At last came the day
Maudie heard the whale say,
"That's France in the distance, you know."
As Maudie laid eyes on
land on the horizon,
he said, "That's as far as I go."

"I'll miss you both awfully,"
their whale friend said softly.
"Please think of me now and again."
And Maudie said sadly,
"I promise you that we
will think of you often, my friend."

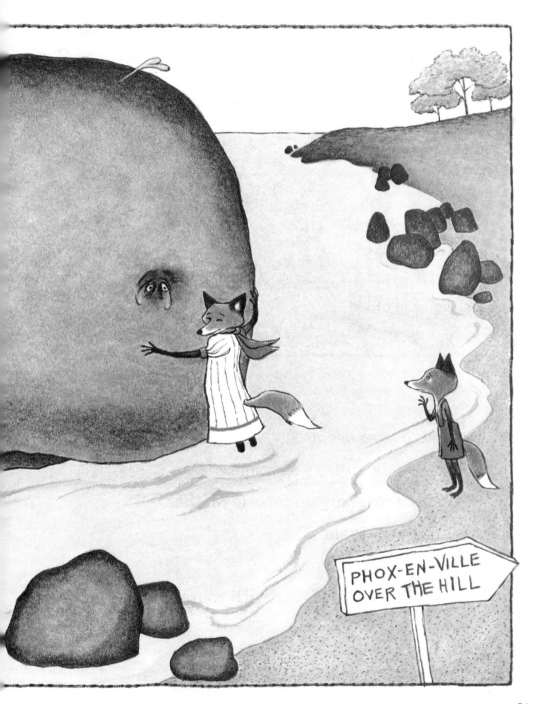

PHOX-EN-VILLE
OVER THE HILL

31

Maude later declared,

"What adventure we've shared,

all because of my promise to Mother.

It just goes to show

how caring can grow,

even when it starts out with your brother!"